I Can Help!

Peggy Perry Anderson

Green Light Readers

HOUGHTON MIFFLIN HARCOURT

BOSTON   NEW YORK

This book is lovingly dedicated to
my grandchildren, Jacob, Céo, and Luke

Library of Congress Cataloging-in-Publication Data
Anderson, Peggy Perry, author, illustrator.
I can help! / by Peggy Perry Anderson.
p. cm. — (Green Light readers. Level 1)
Summary: Although mishaps and near calamities ensue when Joe the frog
"helps" his parents run errands and do chores around the house and yard,
his mother and father have patience and a good sense of humor.
ISBN 978-0-544-52863-5 paper over board
ISBN 978-0-544-52801-7 trade paper
[1. Stories in rhyme. 2. Helpfulness—Fiction. 3. Parent and child—Fiction.
4. Frogs—Fiction.] I. Title.
PZ8.3.A5484Iak 2015
[E]—dc23
2014023628

Manufactured in China
SCP 10 9 8 7 6 5 4 3 2 1

4500535553

I can run errands
with Mommy.

I can show her the big green ball.

I can pick up the clean clothes.

I can look and not touch at all.

I can put mail in the mailbox.

I can sing while we ride in the car.

I can read while we wait for new tires.

I can roam . . .

if I don't go too far.

I can help shop for the groceries.

I can carry bags all by myself.

I can put away oranges and apples.

I can stack the cans on the shelf.

I can do chores with Daddy.

I can hand him a nail or two.

I can reach to put up
the porch swing.

I can paint it the color blue.

I can wash
paint off the
brushes.

I can rake grass
in a heap.

I can move dirt in the garden.

I can pick carrots to eat.

I can toss peas in the salad.

I can share if Daddy wants more.

I can sweep up the cake crumbs.

I can close the dishwasher door.

I can take out the garbage.

I can use these empty jars.

I can do something for Mommy and Daddy.

I can give them the stars!